IT'S SHOWTIME!

A
Pepper
AND
Frannie
Story

CATHERINE LAZAR ODELL

PAGE
STREET
KIDS

Frannie is fancy and free,
and loves to perform for an audience.

Pepper is practical and prepared,
and prefers to play when no one is around.

Pepper and Frannie are best friends,
and they both love a good show.

Frannie is feeling inspired to put on a show of her own.

Pepper agrees to help out behind the scenes.

They don't waste any time.
Frannie can't wait to perform her favorite song in front of everyone.

She works on her costumes,

and her dance moves.

Pepper pays close attention to every detail.

She makes a to-do list,

and fashions the perfect props.

Pepper is very creative.

Frannie wants to shine.

She wants action.

She wants drama.

Pepper helps make it happen.

Frannie still feels like she is forgetting something . . .

Pepper goes over her to-do list
one more time.

Frannie is feeling confident.
This is going to be a fabulous show.

They arrive early the next morning
to set up.

Pepper double-checks the rigging
while Frannie gets in the zone.

They both take a deep breath.

Ready?

Frannie makes a grand entrance, twirling and spinning,
while Pepper puppeteers the props.

Then she reaches for her guitar . . .

Frannie freezes.

She does not remember
the first chord
or the words.

But she tries to keep going.

She changes her costume and
adds some flair to her dance moves.

Then she signals
for more props.

Then she stops.

This is not how Frannie imagined
her first big show.

It is so quiet.

Her knees begin to tremble.

Frannie wishes she could disappear.

Screeeech

Frannie needs backup.
Pepper is nervous but she tries to ignore the audience
and focuses on her friend.

She plays the first chord.

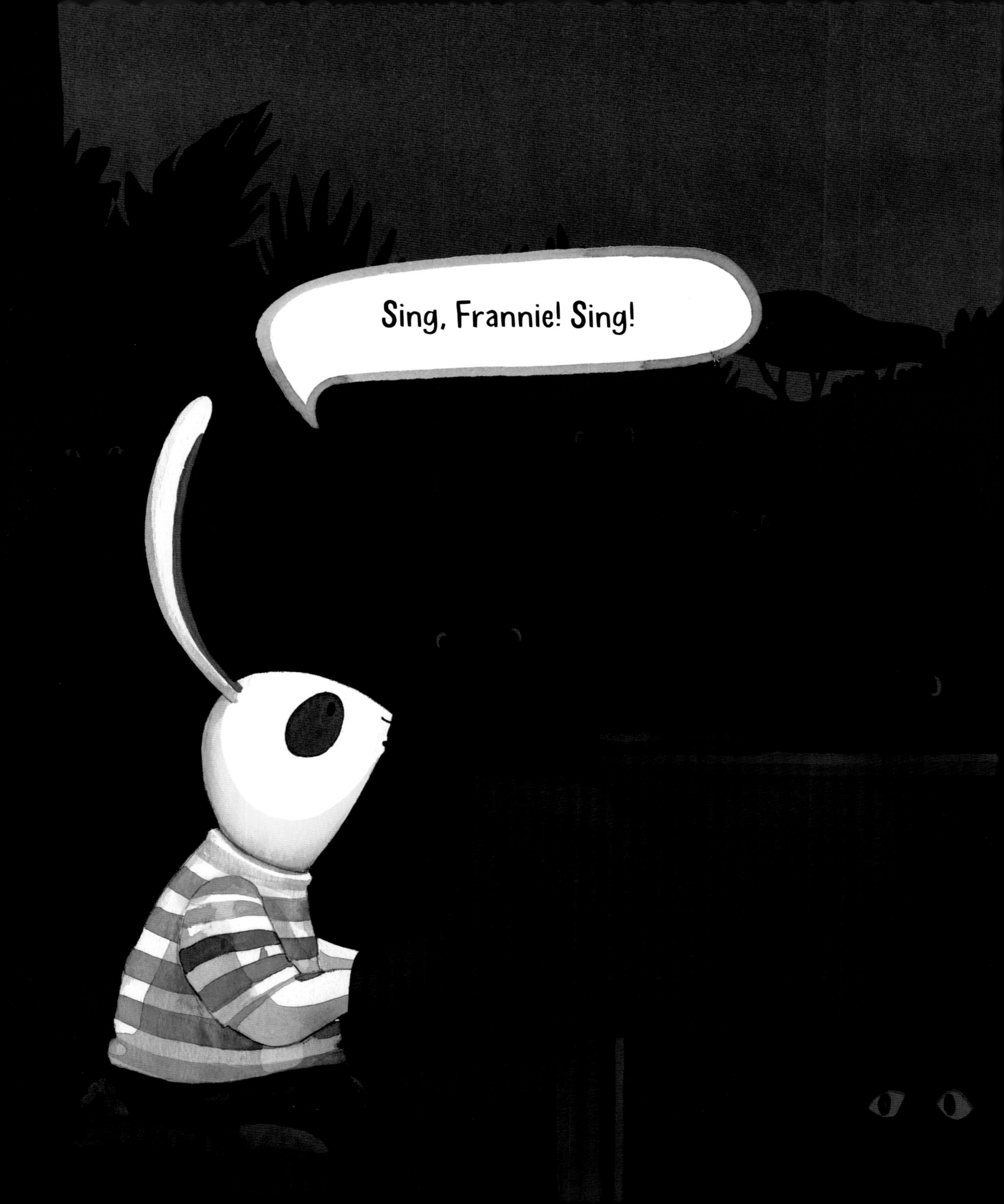
Sing, Frannie! Sing!

Listening to Pepper's perfect piano playing
helps Frannie remember the words.

She takes a deep breath and
starts to sing along.

They lift each other up and their
beautiful music fills the forest.

Together, they shine brighter.

It was a fabulous show after all.

For Mom.

Say it, play it, look at it.

Copyright © 2020 Catherine Lazar Odell
First published in 2020 by Page Street Kids
an imprint of
Page Street Publishing Co.
27 Congress Street, Suite 105
Salem, MA 01970
www.pagestreetpublishing.com

20 21 22 23 24 CCO 5 4 3 2 1

ISBN-13: 978-1-62414-939-9. ISBN-10: 1-62414-939-1
CIP data for this book is available from the Library of Congress.

This book was typeset in Brandon Grotesque.
The illustrations were done in mixed media.

Printed and bound in Shenzhen, Guangdong, China

Page Street Publishing uses only materials from suppliers who are committed
to responsible and sustainable forest management.

Page Street Publishing protects our planet by donating to nonprofits like The Trustees,
which focuses on local land conservation.